Rachel Isadora

Caribbean Dream

PUFFIN BOOKS

W9-DGF-345

To my father

Excerpt from *The Child's Return* reproduced with permission of Curtis Brown Ltd, London,
on behalf of the Estate of Phyllis Shand Allfrey. Copyright Phyllis Shand Allfrey.

PUFFIN BOOKS
Published by the Penguin Group
Penguin Putnam Books for Young Readers,
345 Hudson Street, New York, New York 10014, U.S.A.
Penguin Books Ltd, 80 Strand, London WC2R ORL, England
Penguin Books Australia Ltd, Ringwood, Victoria, Australia
Penguin Books Canada Ltd, 10 Alcorn Avenue, Toronto, Ontario, Canada M4V 3B2
Penguin Books (N.Z.) Ltd, 182-190 Wairau Road, Auckland 10, New Zealand

Penguin Books Ltd, Registered Offices: Harmondsworth, Middlesex, England

First published in the United States of America by G. P. Putnam's Sons,
a division of The Putnam & Grosset Group, 1998
Published by Puffin Books, a division of Penguin Putnam Books for Young Readers, 2002

1 3 5 7 9 10 8 6 4 2

Copyright © Rachel Isadora, 1998

THE LIBRARY OF CONGRESS HAS CATALOGED THE G. P. PUTNAM'S SONS EDITION AS FOLLOWS:
Isadora, Rachel. Caribbean Dream/Rachel Isadora. p. cm.
Summary: A lyrical and evocative dreamscape of the Caribbean.
[1. Caribbean area—Fiction. 2. Dreams—Fiction.] I. Title.
PZ7.1763Car 1998 [E]—dc21 97-49630 CIP AC
ISBN 0-399-23230-3

Puffin Books ISBN 0-698-11944-4

Printed in the United States of America

Except in the United States of America, this book is sold subject to the condition that it shall not,
by way of trade or otherwise, be lent, re-sold, hired out, or otherwise circulated without the publisher's
prior consent in any form of binding or cover other than that in which it is published and without
a similar condition including this condition being imposed on the subsequent purchaser.

I remember a far tall island
floating in cobalt paint
The thought of it is a
childhood dream

—*Phyllis Shand Allfrey*
THE CHILD'S RETURN

Where morning
meets light,
we rise.

Where friends
meet friends,
we smile.

Where sound

meets color,

we hide.

Where waves

meet sand,

we swim.

Where sun

meets water,

we fish.

Where sea

meets sky,

we sail.

Where wind
meets hill,
we run.

Where rain

meets earth,

we splash.

Where darkness
meets light,
we dream.

We dream.